First edition, *Mi piace il cioccolato*, published in Italy by ZOOlibri in 2001
Text and illustrations copyright © ZOOlibri – Reggio Emilia – Italia. All rights reserved.

First published in this edition by Tundra Books, Toronto, 2009
English translation copyright © 2009 by Tundra Books

Published in Canada by Tundra Books,
75 Sherbourne Street, Toronto, Ontario M5A 2P9

Published in the United States by Tundra Books of Northern New York,
P.O. Box 1030, Plattsburgh, New York 12901

Library of Congress Control Number: 2008906708

Library and Archives Canada Cataloguing in Publication

Calì, Davide, 1972-
    I love chocolate / Davide Calì ; illustrations by Evelyn Daviddi.

Translation of: Mi piace il cioccolato.
Interest age level: For ages 2-5.
ISBN 978-0-88776-912-2

    1. Chocolate–Juvenile literature. I. Daviddi, Evelyn II. Title.

TX767.C5C3513 2009   j641.3'374   C2008-903677-8

We acknowledge the financial support of the Government of Canada through the Book Publishing Industry Development Program and that of the Government of Ontario through the Ontario Media Development Corporation's Ontario Book Initiative. We further acknowledge the support of the Canada Council for the Arts and the Ontario Arts Council for our publishing program.

ONTARIO ARTS COUNCIL
CONSEIL DES ARTS DE L'ONTARIO

Design by Leah Springate

Printed and bound in China

1 2 3 4 5 6   14 13 12 11 10 09

I Love Chocolate

Illustrated by

By Davide Calì

Evelyn Daviddi

TUNDRA BOOKS

Why do I love chocolate?

I love chocolate bars

because they

CRUNCH

between my teeth.

And I love *ooey gooey* chocolates because they

MELT

in my mouth.

I love chocolate when
it's full of surprises.
You have to take
a bite to find out
what's inside!

Almonds,
caramel,
nougat,
vanilla cream,
and, best of all,
cherries!

I love chocolate
because it even
looks yummy!

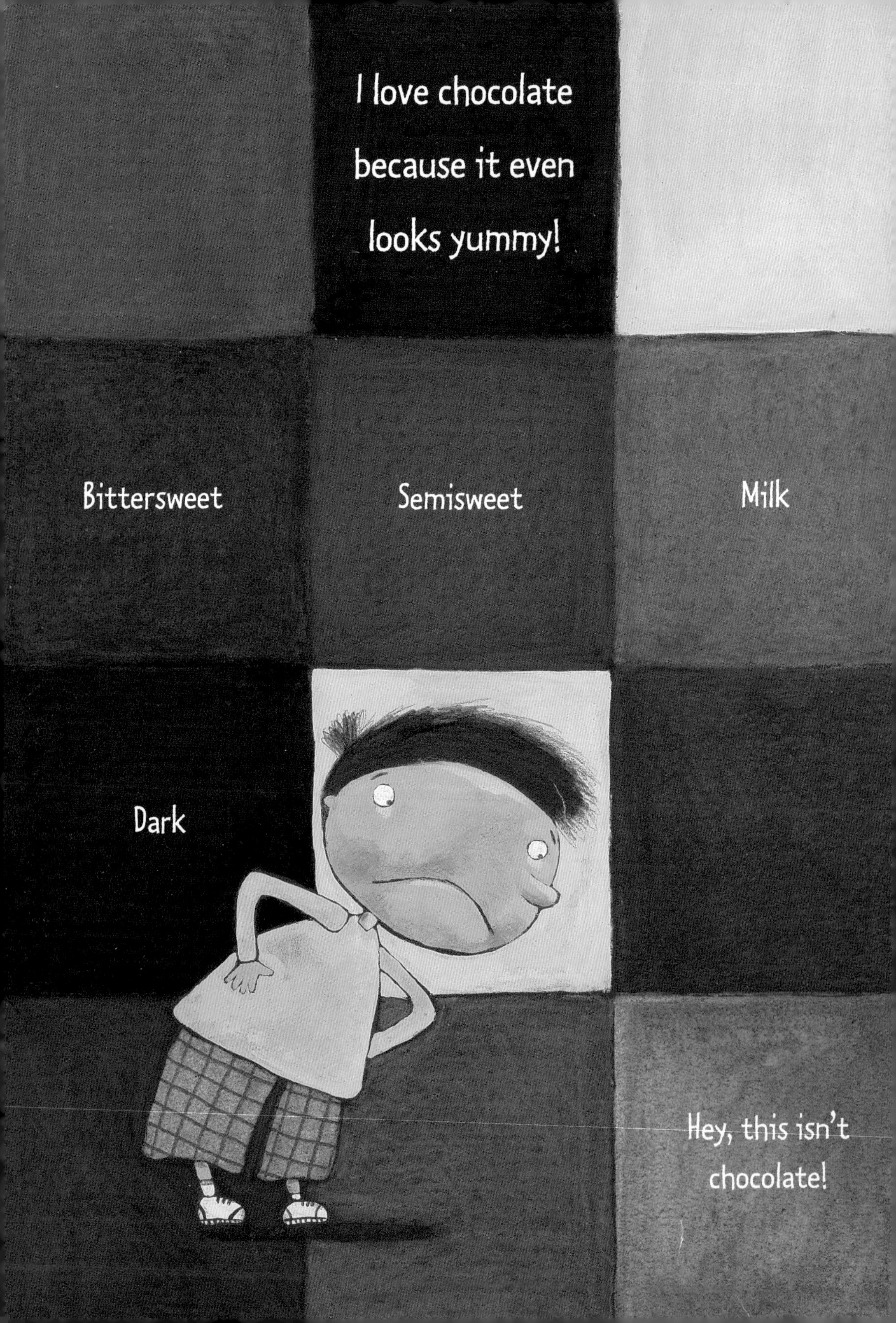

I love **white chocolate** because it reminds me of milk.

I know, **let's share!**

I love chocolate
because it makes
bad times **better**:

Like when someone
needs cheering up after
a bad day at school ...

when the
TV's on the
blink ...

when people get angry ...

when friends don't
seem to care ...

when you're
bored at a
football
game ...

when someone at
day care gets to your
favorite toy car first ...

when you've
been benched ...

when you're
scared of
the dark ...

when you get
chocolate smears
on your best pants ...

I love chocolate

because it makes

every day a

celebration:

On **Monday** because school starts,

or **Tuesday**, when you've made a new friend,

on **Wednesday**
because you
gave your heart,

Wanna
be my
girlfriend?

on **Thursday**
because you
made peace,

on **Friday** because you
made a hurt hurt less,

on **Saturday** because you owned up to breaking Mom's favorite pot,

and on **Sunday** because you made Dad feel better when he couldn't find a place to park.

I love chocolate
because there are so
many ways to enjoy it.
What's your chocolate-
eating **style?**

Are you a **dainty
chocolate
dabbler?**

Are you a **messy chocolate musher?**

Or a **neat nibbler?**

Do you eat chocolate by the **handful?**

Why do I love chocolate?

Because

it makes my **mouth** happy,

my **tummy** happy,

and my **heart** happy!

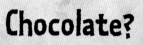

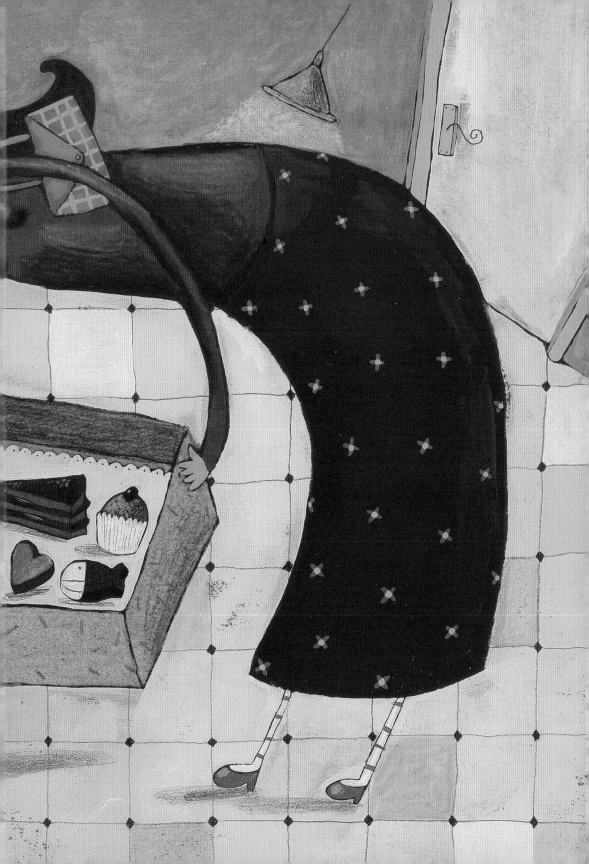